EVERYDAY SCIENCE

Health

To my granddaughter, Megan Kate

Please visit our web site at: www.garethstevens.com
For a free color catalog describing Gareth Stevens Publishing's list of
high-quality books and multimedia programs, call 1-800-542-2595 (USA)
or 1-800-387-3178 (Canada). Gareth Stevens Publishing's fax: (414) 332-3567.

Library of Congress Cataloging-In-Publication Data

Riley, Peter D.
    Health / by Peter Riley.— North American ed.
       p. cm. — (Everyday science)
    Summary: A brief introduction to basic health concepts.
    Includes bibliographical references and index.
    ISBN 0-8368-3715-0 (lib. bdg.)
    1. Health—Juvenile literature. [1. Health.] I. Title.
RA776.5.R536   2003
613—dc21   2003042733

This North American edition first published in 2004 by
Gareth Stevens Publishing
A World Almanac Education Group Company
330 West Olive Street, Suite 100
Milwaukee, Wisconsin 53212 USA

Original text © 2003 by Peter Riley. Images © 2003 by Franklin Watts.
First published in 2003 by Franklin Watts, 96 Leonard Street, London, EC2A 4XD, England.
This U.S. edition copyright © 2004 by Gareth Stevens, Inc.

Series Editor: Sarah Peutrill
Art Director: Jonathan Hair
Designer: Ian Thompson
Photography: Ray Moller (unless otherwise credited)
Photo Researcher: Diana Morris
Gareth Stevens Editor: Carol Ryback
Gareth Stevens Designer: Melissa Valuch

Picture Credits:
(t) top, (b) bottom, (c) center, (l) left, (r) right
Photofushion: /Tim Dub, p. 18(c); /David Montford, p. 21(cr).
SPL: /Dr. Gary Gaugler, p. 14(c).

The original publisher thanks the following children for modeling for this book: Amber Barkhouse, Reece Calvert, Shani-e Cox,
Chantelle Daniel, Ammar Duffus, Alex Green, Harry Johal, and Emily Scott.

Printed in Hong Kong

1 2 3 4 5 6 7 8 9 07 06 05 04 03

EVERYDAY SCIENCE

Health

Written by Peter Riley

Gareth Stevens Publishing
A WORLD ALMANAC EDUCATION GROUP COMPANY

About This Book

Everyday Science is designed to encourage children to think about their everyday world in a scientific way, by examining cause and effect through close observation and discussing what they have seen. Here are some tips to help you get the most from **Health**.

- This book introduces the basic concepts of keeping healthy and some of the vocabulary associated with them, such as energy, exercise, and the comparison of clean and cleanest, and it prepares children for more advanced learning about health.

- On page 10, be sure to emphasize that it is natural for different people to grow at different rates.

- On pages 11, 15, and 21, children are invited to predict the results of a particular action or test. Discuss the reason for any answers they give in some depth before turning the page.

- On page 12, discuss healthy meals and explain how to exchange food that a child will not eat for a similar food that a child will eat.

- On page 13, ask children what to add to each meal shown in order to improve it and make it more healthy.

- On pages 13, 17, and 25, children are invited to use their general knowledge to make a prediction about staying healthy.

- Page 18 provides children with an opportunity to relate anecdotes about losing baby teeth and what it was like until their adult teeth grew into place.

- Page 25 requires a certain level of sensitivity regarding the health circumstances of the children involved. Emphasize the role of the adult in taking medications.

Contents

A **Healthy** Body

A healthy body helps you stay well and happy.

Here are some ways to help keep your body healthy.

Eat and drink a variety of healthy foods.

Stay
clean.

Exercise.

Sleep.

Are you staying healthy?

Food for Energy

Your body works hard all the time.
You use energy for everything you do.
You get your energy from food.

bread

rice

pasta

potatoes

oats

Foods like these give your body
large amounts of energy.

Food for Health

You need to eat different kinds of fruits and vegetables to stay healthy.

Which of these healthy foods do you like to eat?

What vegetables are on this skewer?

Food for  Growth

Every person grows at his or her own rate. These foods help people grow.

cheese

lentils

beans

eggs

fish

meat

What do you eat to help you grow?

You need to eat food that gives you
energy, food that keeps you healthy,
and food that helps you grow.
You also need to drink plenty
of water and other liquids.

Sam and Hannah
want to make a
healthy meal.

What healthy foods could they choose?
Turn the page to find out.

Healthy Meals

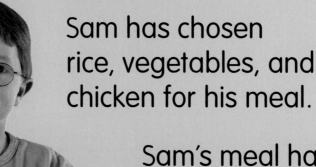

Sam has chosen rice, vegetables, and chicken for his meal.

Sam's meal has food for energy, food for staying healthy, and food for growth.

Here is another healthy meal.

potato, cheese, salad

Hannah has chosen a meal of beef and cheese for growth.

She also needs to choose some food for energy and some food for staying healthy.

Here is a meal that has food for staying healthy and food for energy, but no food for growth.

banana, potato

What should you always do before you eat?
Turn the page to find out.

Keeping Clean

You should always wash your hands before eating.

You should also always wash your hands after using the restroom.

Washing your hands washes away tiny living things called germs.

Some germs can make you sick if they get into your body. Germs can get into your body from dirty hands.

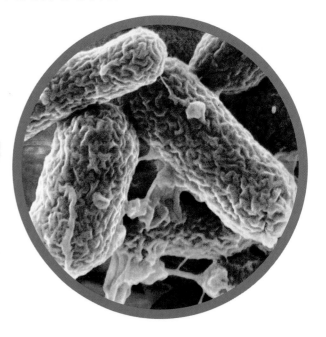

You need a powerful microscope to see germs!

Paul, Katie, and Nicole have dirty hands.
They all wash their hands for 15 seconds.

Katie uses
cold water.

Paul uses cold
water and soap.

Nicole uses warm
water and soap.

Who do you think will have the cleanest hands?
Turn the page to find out.

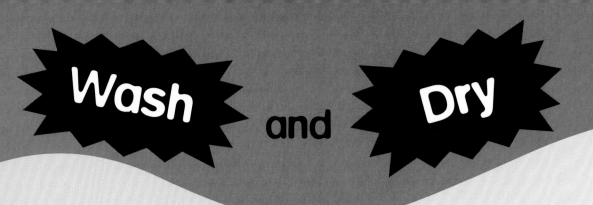

Wash and Dry

Nicole's hands are the cleanest.

Warm water and soap are best for washing your hands.

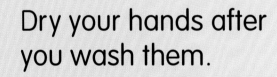

Dry your hands after you wash them.

You need to keep your whole body clean.

Your skin makes a salty liquid called sweat to keep you cool. Sweat makes your skin dirty. Germs can live in dirt on your skin.

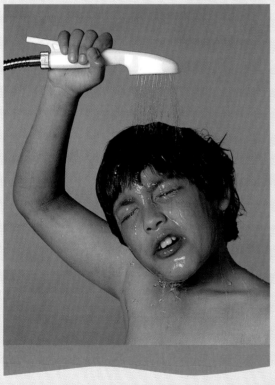

Washing your whole body every day gets rid of any germs that might be living in the dirt on your skin.

What else on your body should you clean every day? Turn the page to find out.

Teeth

You need to clean your teeth every day.
Brushing your teeth keeps them healthy.
Healthy teeth help you bite and chew your food.

Humans grow two sets
of teeth, called baby teeth
and adult teeth. You grew
your baby teeth when
you were about six
months old.

When you are about six
years old, you start to
lose your baby teeth.
Bigger, adult teeth grow
in their place.

Here are three ways to keep your teeth healthy.

1. Brush your teeth
after every meal
and before you
go to sleep.

2. Do not eat a lot
of foods that have
sugar in them.

3. Visit your
dentist twice
a year.

Exercise

Exercise helps your body stay healthy.

Exercise helps your joints stay healthy.

Exercise helps your muscles stay healthy and get stronger.

You can get exercise in many ways.
Hannah and Alex are on their way to school.

Hannah is walking.

Alex is going to
ride in a car.

Who is getting more exercise?
Turn the page to find out.

Body Parts

Hannah is exercising her arms and legs as she walks to school.

Tom

Sophie

Sarah

Which parts of their bodies are Tom, Sophie, and Sarah exercising?

Taking a Break

Sam and Nicole have been playing outside for an hour.

Why do you think they need to take a break to eat a snack and drink some liquids?

Feeling Sick

Sometimes you feel sick.

Sometimes you feel hot, or your body aches. Sometimes you may cough or sneeze.

Sometimes you may need to visit a doctor.

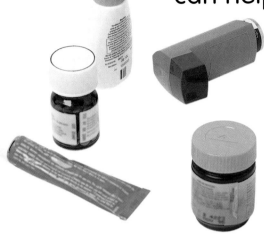

Sometimes medicine can help you feel better.

Medicine should only be taken in a certain amount, called a dose of medicine, at one time. Do not take a dose of medicine yourself. Make sure that only an adult gives you a dose of medicine.

What else can you do to feel better?
Turn the page to find out.

Sleep

You need lots of sleep to stay healthy and to get better when you are sick.

Sleep helps our bodies rest. It helps give us energy and makes us feel healthy.

If you do not get enough sleep, you may feel tired and grumpy.

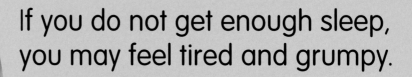

If you get enough sleep, you will have plenty of energy, and you will feel good.

How long do you sleep? Make your own table like this one and fill it in.

day	wake up	lights out
Sunday		
Monday		
Tuesday		
Wednesday		
Thursday		
Friday		
Saturday		

Useful Words

dentist: a type of doctor who has learned how to help you keep your teeth healthy and who also knows how to fix any problems you may have with your teeth.

doctor: a person whose job is to know why you get sick and how to make you feel better.

dose: an amount of medicine that is taken at one time.

energy: the power you get from the food you eat.

exercise: to actively move your muscles and body around.

germs: tiny living things that are too small to see but can make you feel sick.

healthy: full of strength and energy.

joints: points in the body where two bones meet and where your body can bend or twist.

liquids: fluid materials, such as water, that take the shape of the containers holding them.

lentils: dried seeds that look and taste like beans.

medicine: a liquid, tablet, or spray that an adult may give you when you are sick in order to make you feel better.

microscope: a tool that makes very tiny objects look bigger.

muscles: soft parts inside your body that help you move.

sweat: a salty liquid that comes out of your skin when your body is hot.

Some Answers

Here are some answers to the questions asked in this book. If you had different answers, you may be right, too. Talk over your answers with other people and see if you can explain why they are right.

page 9   The vegetables on the skewer include mushrooms, zucchini, red peppers, and onions.

page 10   Cheese, eggs, lentils, beans, meat, and fish all help you grow. These foods can be prepared in many different ways. For example, eggs can be fried, scrambled, boiled, or made into an omelette. You can eat cheese in a sandwich or as a sauce over a hot meal. Beans and lentils are delicious in soups. Different types of meat and fish can be prepared in many different ways. You can also combine these foods with other healthy foods in a salad or a casserole. Try something new!

page 22   Tom is exercising both his arms and legs, but mainly his legs. Sophie is exercising her legs. Sarah is exercising her arms.

page 23   Sam and Nicole need to take a break so they can eat a snack to replace the energy that they have used up while playing outside. They also need to drink liquids to replace the water from their bodies that they lost through sweat.

For More Information

More Books to Read

- *A Healthy Body. Safe and Sound* (series)
  Angela Royston
  (Heinemann Library)

- *Eat Healthy, Feel Great*
  William Sears and Martha Sears
  (Little, Brown & Company)

- *What to Expect When You Go to the Dentist.*
  What to Expect Kids (series). Heidi Murkoff
  (HarperFestival)

Web Sites

- BrainPOP: Nutrition
  www.brainpop.com/health/growthanddevelopment/nutrition

- Your Gross and Cool Body
  yuckykids.discovery.com/noflash/body*index.html*

Index